This dragon book belongs to:
......Tana Young..................

Virtual Learning Dragon
My Dragon Books - Volume 39
Written by Steve Herman

Copyright © 2020 by Digital Golden Solutions LLC.
Published by DG Books Publishing, an imprint of Digital Golden Solutions LLC.

All rights reserved. No part of this publication may be reproduced, distributed, or transmitted in any form or by any means, including photocopying, recording, or other electronic or mechanical methods, without the prior written permission of the publisher, except in the case of brief quotations embodied in critical reviews and certain other noncommercial uses permitted by copyright law.

Information contained within this book is for entertainment and educational purposes only. Although the author and publisher have made every effort to ensure that the information in this book was correct at press time, the author and publisher do not assume and hereby disclaim any liability to any party for any loss, damage, or disruption caused by errors or omissions, whether such errors or omissions result from negligence, accident, or any other cause.

ISBN: 978-1-64916-070-6 (paperback)
ISBN: 978-1-64916-071-3 (hardcover)

www.MyDragonBooks.com

First Edition: September 2020
10 9 8 7 6 5 4 3 2 1

We see our teacher on the screen –
she tells us what to do
Like work a page of math
and then read a book or two.

First he made a sandwich, then opened up a can of pop; He would have eaten ice cream, too, but Mother told him, "STOP!"

STOP!

"I don't like doing school like this;
it's not any fun!
When will this virus end?
I can't wait until it's done!"

Diggory Doo apologized about the way he'd acted, But school at home was hard because he got distracted.

My dragon is more mindful now when he is on the screen,
And never takes his laptop places he should not be seen!

Now that he applies himself, Diggory's doing fine;
He's discovered school is also fun, even when online.

Made in the USA
Monee, IL
09 September 2020